STEVE YOUNG

YOUNG

8

Forever Young

Text by Steve Young with Greg Brown • Illustrated by Doug Keith

Greg Brown lives in Bothell, Washington, with his wife Stacy and two children. Greg is the founder of the Positively for Kids series of children's books with athletes. His book with Troy Aikman, *Things Change*, was a national bestseller, as was his book with Cal Ripken Jr., *Count Me In*. Greg is also the co-author of *Be the Best You Can Be* with Kirby Puckett and *Patience Pays* with Edgar Martinez. Brown regularly speaks at schools and can be reached at his internet address: pfkgb@aol.com.

Doug Keith provided the illustrations for the best-selling children's book *Things Change* with Troy Aikman and *Count Me In* with Cal Ripken Jr. His illustrations have appeared in national magazines such as *Sports Illustrated for Kids*, greeting cards, and books. Keith can be reached at his internet address: atozdk@aol.com.

Steve Young has donated all of his royalties from the sale of this book to his Forever Young Foundation, which encourages the development, strength, and education of children and families.

Published by Taylor Publishing Company
1550 West Mockingbird Lane
Dallas, Texas 75235

Designed by David Timmons

Library of Congress Cataloging-in-Publication Data

Young, Steve, 1961–
  Forever Young / by Steve Young with Greg Brown ; illustrations by Doug Keith
    p.   cm.
  Summary: An autobiography describing the personal life and football career of the quarterback who led the San Francisco 49ers to a Super Bowl win in 1995.
  ISBN 0-87833-930-2
  1. Young, Steve, 1961—Juvenile literature. 2. Football player—United States—Biography—Juvenile literature. 3. San Francisco 49ers (Football team)—Juvenile literature. [1. Young, Steve, 1961–   . 2. Football players.]
  I. Brown, Greg. II. Keith, Doug, ill. III. Title.
  GV939.Y69A3   1996
  796.332'092—dc20
  [B]   96-18835
                                                                      CIP
                                                                       AC

Printed in the United States of America
10 9 8 7 6 5 4 3 2 1

Background photo: Carlin/Archive Photos. Steve as adult: Steve Hathaway.

My name is Steve Young, and I play quarterback for the San Francisco 49ers. I have written this book to talk with you about life's unpredictable journeys. Everyone is faced with different hardships; how we confront these challenges will determine the kind of person we will become.

Some people say winning a big game like the Super Bowl determines success, while others say you're only successful if you make a lot of money.

Well, I have played on a winning Super Bowl team, and have made more money than I could have ever imagined by playing football.

But I measure my success by other standards.

I know what it's like to fear the unknown, to want to quit, and to feel worthless. I also know the victory in overcoming struggles.

Growing up, I was afraid to spend the night away from home—so I didn't, until I went to college.

I could barely throw the football 20 yards my first year in college, and I wanted to give up.

I was so scared the day I signed to play professional football that I cried. I didn't think that I could ever live up to everyone's expectations.

To me, overcoming obstacles defines success even more than winning a Super Bowl.

My story begins in 1961 when I was born in Salt Lake City, Utah, to my loving parents, LeGrande and Sherry Young.

The first of five children, I had a head start on sports. I dressed as a football player my first Halloween at age two and already could do pushups.

By my third birthday I could dribble a basketball!

My brother Mike was born on my second birthday. Two years later came sister Melissa. Brother Tom is eight years younger, and I was 17 when Jim was born.

My parents gave us a great childhood. We played from sun up to sun down.

Mike and I did everything together, from looking for butterflies to just goofing around.

My world was all fun and games, that is until I went to second grade.

For some reason, going to second grade at Meadow Moor Elementary School upset me. I don't remember why. I liked learning in school; I just didn't want to leave home and my family.

My parents, of course, worried about what bothered me. Nobody could figure it out.

Finally, Mom said she would go to school with me and sit in my class. She did that every day for the first couple of weeks. Soon my worry disappeared, and I didn't need Mom to go to school with me anymore.

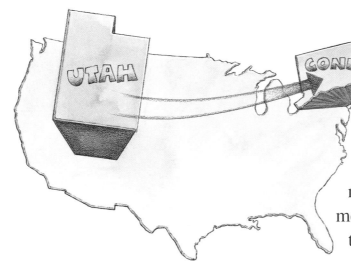

The summer after third grade, my family moved to Greenwich, Connecticut, because Dad, an attorney, changed jobs.

We moved into a neighborhood filled with kids. I made new friends and spent many hours outside riding bikes and playing games and sports at the nearby school field.

Because I was one of the younger kids in the neighborhood, some of the older, bigger guys pushed me around. I talked my way out of a lot of fights, and to this day I have never punched anyone.

Seeing bullies pick on weaker kids upset me. I wanted to stand up for them; however, sometimes I didn't have the courage.

Despite my concern for other kids, for some reason, I was not as caring with my brother's feelings. We were competitive about everything.

Even climbing into the "way back" of our station wagon became a race. Because I was stronger, I won most of the time. I never wanted Mike to win anything.

Mike kept trying to outdo me though, and soon he found things he could do better than me—like kite flying and fishing.

One time we went fishing together, and I cast my line and accidentally hooked Mike's ear. We ran home in a panic, but Mom calmly unhooked my catch of the day.

Mike and I grew up with a special connection. We shared a bedroom and we were both born on October 11th.

Mom would have two birthday parties, one in the front of the house and the other in back. It was sometimes hard to share my birthday.

As brothers sometimes do, we had our arguments. One time I was teasing Mike by saying nobody in the family liked him. I said even our family dog, J.J., liked me better.

Mike's anger grew until out of frustration he kicked a hole in the wall. When Dad came home, I got in trouble for it because I was the oldest and should have known not to tease Mike so much.

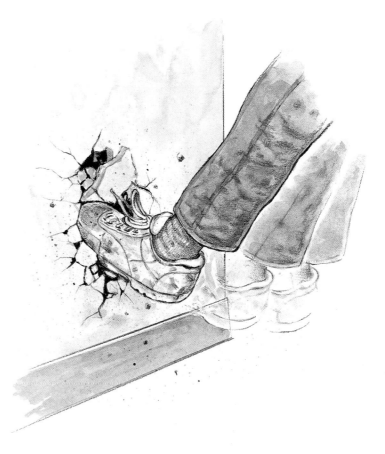

Most of the time, however, everyone got along just fine. I remember spending days in our unfinished basement during the winter months playing with my brothers, sister and friends. Hide-and-seek in the dark was one of our favorite games.

We played hockey and other sports downstairs, but mostly we loved building forts with a bunch of old mattresses my parents stored in our basement.

When I was 10, a neighborhood friend and I decided we would try riding unicycles. Balancing on one wheel seemed impossible at first.

Learning to sit took a week. Learning to pedal took about a month. Pedal… fall…pedal…fall…pedal…fall. The padded seat hit the pavement so many times the ends wore down to the metal.

Once we mastered one full pedal, we quickly learned to keep our balance. My friend and I became so skilled on unicycles we could play basketball on them. We were paid five dollars each to put on halftime shows at the high school basketball games.

To this day, I can hop on any unicycle and ride.

I also loved riding bicycles. Many friends had "Stingray" bikes back then, and I told my parents I wanted one.

My parents made a deal with me: If I earned half the cost of the bike, they would pay the rest.

That was not the answer I wanted. I didn't understand why Dad made us earn our own money and work summer jobs to help buy things we wanted.

I really wanted that bike however, so I started delivering afternoon newspapers to make money.

I saved and saved. The day I plopped down my bag of money for a new purple Schwinn Stingray gave me an unforgettable feeling of accomplishment.

I washed that bike every day and parked it next to my bed for months.

Waiting to buy my bike helped me understand the value of money.

As I grew older, I started playing organized sports. Other players were taller and stronger, but I was a fast runner.

I played running back during little league football. One of my most embarrassing moments happened when Mom ran onto the field during a game.

Someone from the Belhaven Buzzards tackled me illegally by my neck and dazed me. Dad rushed out to check on me, but Mom sprinted to the tackler. She picked him off the ground by his jersey and shouted: "Don't neck tackle!"

Mom and I were teased about that incident for years. When someone tackled me roughly in high school, family friends sitting near Mom would say, "Go out there and get 'em, Sherry."

Most sports came naturally to me, except for swimming. Melissa competed on the swim team, but when I tried out for the Boys' Club team, I couldn't swim even one length of the pool.

For some strange reason, I refused to open my eyes underwater. I zigged and zagged in my lane and my arms kept hitting the floating lane markers. I'd hammer those markers and get so tired I thought I'd drown. Swimming a lap seemed to take hours.

"You've got to watch where you're going," Dad said after he watched me struggle.

"I know, but I can't," I said with defeat.

Finally, Dad suggested, "Maybe you should try another sport."

Football, baseball and basketball were my favorites. By the time I turned 13, my reputation of being a good athlete caught some attention. That spring the best baseball team in my age group drafted me.

Unfortunately, I did not get a single hit the first few weeks of the season. My parents encouraged me, saying everyone has slumps.

But my slump kept going and going. Soon I was 0-for-30. I even tried to bunt for a hit. Nothing worked.

Baseball became a never-ending nightmare. I worried about going hitless the entire season.

"I don't know what's wrong," I'd say to my parents, almost in tears.

I remember Mom trying to cheer me up by saying, "Maybe you should try tennis."

This time I wasn't going to quit. I hung in there. Toward the end of the season, I finally got a break and made a couple of hits. That winter, with Dad's help, I made a commitment to improve my hitting.

Throughout the winter, Dad and I put on our heavy parkas and went down to the school and hit baseballs.

It didn't matter how cold it was or how much snow covered the ground. Every weekend we would practice. My confidence returned by the next spring and my hitting improved.

Those winter batting practices taught me that hard work does pay off and it also taught me that spending time with me was one of the ways Dad showed his love for me.

Dad was strict with us, and, like all families, we had our disagreements. But if I didn't always agree with Dad, I still followed his rules. One time I didn't pay attention to his warnings and it almost cost me a few fingers.

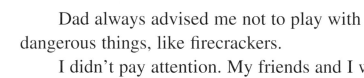

Dad always advised me not to play with dangerous things, like firecrackers.

I didn't pay attention. My friends and I would light firecrackers and see how far we could count before throwing them. Guess what happened one time?

I lit the fuse. "One thousand one; one thousand two; one thousand"—boom!

The firecracker exploded in my left hand. I thought it blew off some fingers it hurt so much.

Fortunately, huge blood blisters on my pointer finger and thumb were the only damage, besides my pride.

I missed a week of sports while my hand healed, and Dad reminded me every day, "How many times do I have to tell you about tempting danger? You have to be smarter than that."

The whole time I kept thinking, "I can't believe I did that. I am such an idiot."

Sometimes even though our parents' advice is hard to accept, they know what is best for us. Believe me, we all do stupid things. The important thing is to learn from our mistakes.

STUDENT NO.	STUDENT NAME	SCHOOL YEAR	SEX	HOME ROOM	COUNSELOR	HOUSE	GRADE	CUMULATIVE RECORD ABSENT	TARDY
953330	YOUNG J STEVEN	77-78	M		HARDING	B	10		

COURSE	SEC.	SUBJECT	TEACHER	PER.	ROOM NO.	SEM.	DAYS MET	1ST	2ND	3RD	4TH	FINAL	CREDITS
06141	PHYS ED		XXX	01	GYM	8					A		
06121	PHYS ED		XXX	01	GYM	2			A		A	A	.25
06131	PHYS ED		XXX	01	GYM	4				P		P	.25
06101	PHYS ED		XXX	01	GYM	1		P				P	.25
24603	HON ALG 2		MIL	03	405	F		B1	A1	A1	A1	A1	4.00
50101	FRENCH10A		MON	04	205	F		B1	A1	A1	A1	A1	4.00
13021	CHEMISTRY		FLT	05	556	F		A1	A1	A1	A1	A1	4.00
41007	AM HIS 10		SMH	06	114	F		A1	A1	A1	A1	A1	4.00
30101	ENG 113		HOP	07	112	3		A1	A1			A1	2.00
30121	ENG 123		HOP	07	112	C				A1	B1	A1	2.00

STUDENT ACHIEVEMENT REPORT

GRADE STANDARD	INDIVIDUAL EFFORT
A - EXCELLENT	1 - EXCELLENT
B - ABOVE AVERAGE	2 - AVERAGE
C - AVERAGE	3 - UNSATISFACTORY
D - BELOW AVERAGE	4 - CONDITIONAL
E - FAILURE	5 - PARENT CONFERENCE REQUESTED
F - CREDIT AUDIT	
G - WITHDRAWN	
H - MEDICAL EXCUSE	
I - INCOMPLETE	

P - PASSED

TO THE PARENTS:

THIS REPORTING FORM SERVES AS OUR BASIC COMMUNICATION WITH YOU CONCERNING THE PROGRESS OF YOUR CHILD. IT IS IN YOUR CHILD'S INTEREST THAT YOU COMMUNICATE WITH US WHEN YOU IDENTIFY A PROBLEM. WE WELCOME YOUR CONTACTING THE TEACHERS INVOLVED, THE GUIDANCE COUNSELOR, OR MYSELF.

SINCERELY

JOHN BIRD

HEADMASTER

4TH MARKING PERIOD GRADE POINT AVERAGE   4.000

PREVIOUS CREDITS

TOTAL CUMULATIVE CREDITS

NOTE * INDIVIDUAL EFFORT OF 6 OR MORE REPRESENTS DAYS ABSENT, 9 MEANING 9 OR MORE DAYS ABSENT.

I enjoyed school and always wanted to learn more and be in the toughest classes. I worked hard not to make many mistakes. I earned mostly A's as long as I can remember, but it wasn't easy.

Finding time to study took planning. Our family awoke at 5 a.m. on most days to go to church before school. Then after school I had football, basketball or baseball practice.

Being in the most challenging classes and being an athlete gave me the chance to make friends with many different people: some smarter than others, some more athletic. I found friends who had all types of interests and talents, and I'm still friends with many of them today.

One of my best friends growing up didn't like to play team sports. Dave VanBlerkom lived in my neighborhood and some kids called him a nerd because he was the smartest guy in the class.

We collected stamps, coins and baseball cards together.

In sixth grade, we were in the hallway getting ready for class when a bully started calling Dave names. He started crying.

I pushed the kid away and his head accidentally banged into a locker, causing his ear to bleed.

Afterward I realized that we should have ignored the bully and walked away, but I lost my temper for the moment. That was the closest I have ever come to being in a fist fight.

In junior high school I moved from running back to quarterback. We ran the wishbone offense, which meant I didn't throw the ball much. That was lucky for my teammates because I could not throw well.

I could barely throw it 20 yards because I couldn't figure out how to make the ball spiral.

My sophomore season in high school I threw one of my most embarrassing passes during a morning junior varsity game. Our Greenwich Cardinals team

was struggling, and I threw six interceptions. The worst came when the ball slipped off my hand as I threw it. The ball fluttered in a high rainbow arc as players gathered around underneath. You guessed it, the other team caught it.

The varsity coach, Mike Ornato, was watching the game from the stands. We desperately wanted to impress him. Coach Ornato entered our locker room after the game and declared, "This is the worst group of athletes I've ever seen in my life!"

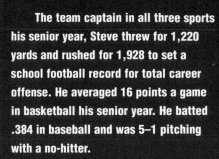

Coach Ornato's words embarrassed and motivated us at the same time. We decided as a team to prove our coach wrong and worked hard during the summer to get in shape for football.

My senior year, we made it to the county championship game, going farther than most people thought we would. We used a run-oriented option offense, which was fine with me. I disliked throwing the football in public because I still couldn't throw it far.

I participated in many memorable games in high school; however, my basketball coach, Garland Allen, taught me the best sports memories go beyond the games.

My sophomore year we had a highly recruited basketball player. Many college coaches watched our games, which made us all nervous because we didn't want to mess up.

Coach Allen called us together and told us to relax and let the future take care of itself. He said playing sports is about having fun and making friendships.

Greenwich Times

The friends I made in school were important to me. My faith grew in importance, too. By my junior year, I had to make some tough choices.

Everyone must choose what they believe is best for themselves. I chose not to drink alcohol in high school, and still don't. Some friends decided they wanted to drink.

At first I felt awkward saying "no thanks." But quickly everyone knew how I felt and no one bothered me about not drinking. If my friends had a beer, I would have a glass of milk.

One night after a football game, we all went to a party. Some started a contest to see who could drink a glass of beer the fastest. I played along, only I drank a glass of milk.

After that, every party I went to people would have milk ready for me to drink. I guess it showed they respected my decision.

Friends who try to pressure you into doing what you believe is wrong are not really friends at all.

Before I knew it, my senior year ended and it was time to go off to college. Brigham Young University, named after my great-great-great grandfather, offered me a football scholarship. I didn't pick BYU, however, because my father played football there or because of my relation to Brigham Young.

I chose BYU because I had relatives and family friends who lived in the Salt Lake City area. I figured Utah would be a home away from home.

Until I left for BYU, I had never spent the night at friends' homes, even though friends stayed at our house all the time. I had an odd fear of sleeping away from my family. I missed out on a lot of fun because I was just too scared to try. I knew it was time to face this fear even though it was hard to say goodbye to family and friends.

I didn't unpack my bags that first semester at school and called home almost every night. Slowly, I began to feel comfortable away from home.

The Young family.

LeGrande "Grit" Young, BYU's top scorer in '55 and leading rusher in '59

The first day of BYU football practice I realized I could not throw as well as the other quarterbacks. I began at the back of the line with seven quarterbacks ahead of me.

I did not make a good first impression, either. On the first snap during my first BYU practice, I dropped back to throw and tripped over my feet. Everyone laughed at me.

Being last in line meant I was the third-string junior-varsity quarterback. They rotated the JV starters, and on the third week, I prepared for my turn. Before

the game, however, a coach told me a different player would start because his father was in town to see him play.

I figured I'd never get my chance to play. I called home and told my parents I wanted to quit and come home.

"You can quit, but you can't come home," Dad said.

Dad's tough-love response helped me understand taking the easy way out is seldom the best way.

Waiting my turn became all too familiar.

Jim McMahon led the nation in passing at BYU my first two years at school.

That first year, I watched him closely, studying every throwing movement. We had the same build, so I copied his throwing style.

Almost immediately, I started to throw better. I mastered the spiral and accuracy. Discovering this new gift was thrilling, and I worked harder to improve.

That winter the BYU coaches decided my speed could help the team more than my arm, so they switched me to defensive back. Before my sophomore season, however, a new quarterback coach was willing to give me a second try.

I worked my way to backup for McMahon, who set 72 NCAA passing records before moving on to an NFL career and a Super Bowl victory with the Bears. I watched and learned, knowing that after he graduated I would get my chance.

I earned the starting quarterback job my junior season. Following McMahon was a tough situation.

Mike

Tom

Expectations were high and immediately people compared me to McMahon.

I remember walking in downtown Provo after our 8–4 season and hearing fans say, "Steve Young sucks."

Those types of comments hurt me deeply. I knew criticism came with playing quarterback, but I wasn't prepared for the harsh words thrown at me. It was only the beginning.

My brother Mike followed my footsteps as a quarterback in high school and decided to attend BYU and play football. It was great having Mike in Provo with me.

Jim

Melissa

Three Young brothers all played quarterback at Greenwich High School and BYU. Mike and Tom both threw for more yards than Steve in high school and eventually became starters at BYU. Injuries hampered Mike's career and his interest turned to medicine. He is now an emergency room doctor. Tom started in the Aloha Bowl and played football in Finland. He is the executive director of Steve's "Forever Young" foundation. Jim broke the quarterback streak by playing linebacker in high school and will graduate from Greenwich High in 1997. Melissa also went to BYU and competed on the swim and track teams. She works for a cosmetics company.

My senior season started with a loss, but we finished winning 11 straight games.

We ended with a victory in the Holiday Bowl. I couldn't have written a better ending to my college football career. I received several awards, but most of all I felt proud about how I proved to myself I could play the game.

The National Football League's Cincinnati Bengals told me that they would select me with the very first pick in the draft. At the time, a competing league, called the United States Football League, was trying to convince top college players to join their spring-time league.

Thanks to the hard work of my new attorney

AP/Doug Pizac

and agent, Leigh Steinberg, the Los Angeles Express offered me more money than anyone had ever been offered to play football. The Bengals had a veteran quarterback. I figured I'd play sooner in the USFL and learn more from L.A.'s veteran coaches.

After much soul searching, I signed my first professional contract with the Express and instantly became the highest-paid athlete in sports at that time.

I was overwhelmed by the money. On the flight back to Provo, I clutched in my hand a check for more money than I had ever imagined and silently cried. I thought I was the wrong person to receive all this money and attention. Dad had always stressed the importance of earning your worth, and I felt unworthy.

Back at Provo and across the nation, news of my contract upset many people. A headline in a paper said: "Steve Young: What's wrong with sports."

All of a sudden, I felt that life had become complicated. I didn't want all the controversy that came with my new contract.

I thought about backing out of the deal as it came time to go back to Los Angeles.

Dad flew out to Provo.

"You signed a contract, now you have to live up to your commitment," he said.

I knew he was right.

AP/Doug Pizac

Steve and agent Leigh Steinberg.

Wealth moves Young to tears

I purposely didn't let all the money change me. I still drove around the same car I had in college, an old Oldsmobile called, "The Tuna Boat," and shared an apartment with four of my Express team-mates. I made some lifelong friendships with those guys and the coaches taught me much about football.

Still, the USFL would never be the NFL. Attendance at our games dwindled. I sometimes thought I could count the number of people in the stands. It was so quiet I had to whisper in the huddle so the other team couldn't hear me.

By my second season, the Express was almost out of money.

We played our final game at a junior college. On the way, our team bus driver pulled off to the side of the road and refused to move

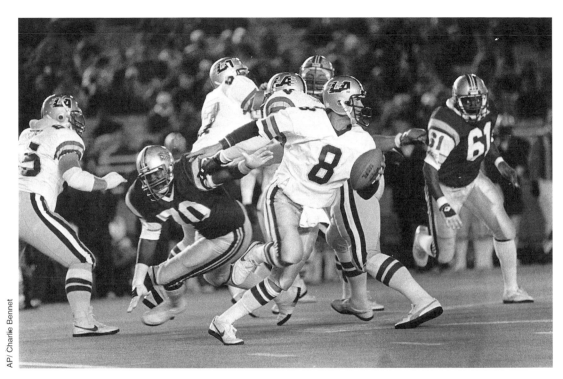

AP/ Charlie Bennet

unless someone paid the $500 the team owed him. We took a collection among the players to pay the driver so we could make it to the game.

Due to injuries, our team ran out of running backs, so I volunteered to fill the position because we had other quarterbacks.

Ironically, my last play in the USFL was at running back.

It seemed a fitting ending to our 3 15 season and my strange two seasons in the USFL.

With the league crumbling, my agent found a way for me to buy out my contract.

That same year I found myself in Tampa Bay playing for the Buccaneers. I didn't care about the team's losing tradition. I just wanted to play.

At midseason, I got my first start. We won the game, but unfortunately not many more.

We played our next game in a snowstorm at Green Bay, Wisconsin. Our team manager forgot our cold-weather gear, so many players actually wore their street clothes under their uniforms!

My first 11 passes were incomplete. I thought I was ruined, that I was going to set an NFL record for most passes without a completion.

So I told my running backs, "On the next play, run right in front of me and I'll shovel it to you so I can get a completion."

I did make a few legitimate passes, but almost suffocated in the process. A Green Bay defender slammed my face into a pile of snow during a tackle. The snow and ice clogged my facemask. I couldn't breathe for a few panic-filled moments until I dug myself out of my own helmet.

I earned my paychecks playing for Tampa Bay, often running for my life. Some criticized me for running too much, saying I wasn't patient enough to be a quality NFL quarterback.

Tampa Bay went 1–10 before I became the starter. We finished 1–4 the rest of the season. My second season with the Bucs wasn't much better. In two seasons, I threw 11 touchdowns and 21 interceptions and won just four games, hardly statistics worth notice.

But San Francisco 49ers coach Bill Walsh did take note. He needed a backup for veteran Joe Montana, believed to have one or two years left in his career.

The Bucs traded me to San Francisco in 1987 and my life changed forever.

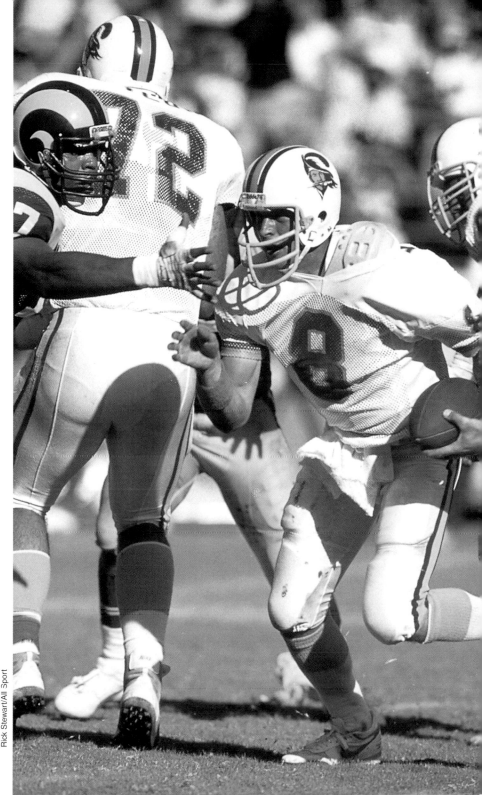

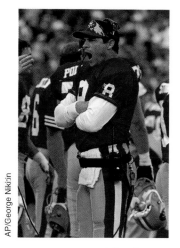

I learned how to throw by watching McMahon, but I learned how to play quarterback by watching Montana.

For four long years, I stood on the sidelines and studied him, waiting.

As I watched Montana lead the 49ers to two of his four Super Bowl wins, I thought I would never start. Each season of limited play tortured me more. I sank into depression.

I'd run sprints after games just to break into a sweat. I even played wide receiver on three plays—anything to get in, to feel useful.

I refused to cash my 49ers paychecks during those seasons because I didn't feel I was earning them, so I stuffed them all into a drawer. I started typing letters to the 49ers president saying he could have his money back. I never sent those letters and eventually cashed the checks. I still felt guilty.

Friends and family urged me to ask for a trade, but I felt I should stay. I enjoyed San Francisco and the team's commitment to being the best.

I just hoped I would get a chance to prove myself.

I went back to BYU during offseasons to earn a law degree and that helped to ease my heavy heart.

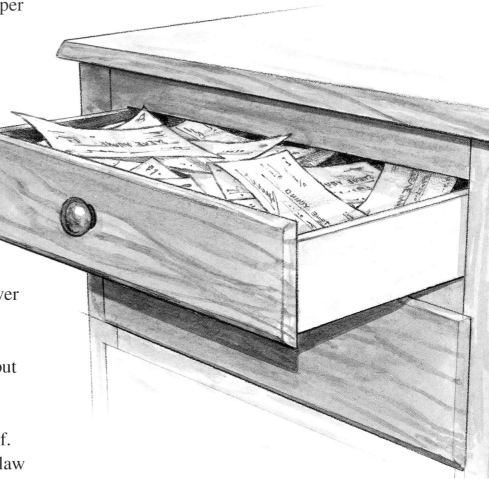

Being around friends and family in the offseason helps me deal with the pressures of playing professional football.

I always visit my family in Connecticut once the football season is over. I enjoy going back to the home where I grew up. My neighborhood brings back great memories, like my old afternoon newspaper route. That route of 50 papers has been passed down from me to each of my siblings. On one trip home I filled in for Tom when he was sick, and another time for Jim.

During one visit, I even became a driving instructor. Melissa had just failed her driving test by backing into another car, so I took her out driving for a few nights. We drove all around the neighborhood backwards so that she would feel confident next time she took the test.

Going home also gave me a chance to build a relationship with Jim. Because our age difference is 17 years, it has been tough for both of us to spend time together. A few summers ago I took Jim, Tom and some friends rafting down the Colorado river. It was great to get to know each other even better.

To me, it's very important to stay in touch with my family, even if it's just an occasional phone call.

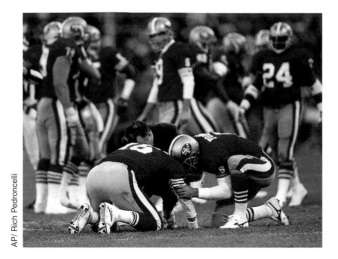

Things began changing in the 1990s. A late-game injury to Montana in the 1990 playoffs thrust me into the game with the lead. But a fumble allowed the New York Giants to come back and win.

The next season I started 10 games but won only five before hurting a knee.

Elbow surgery kept Montana out that season, so in stepped Steve Bono, who won five of the six games he started. We missed the playoffs for the first time in nine years. Fans were furious. They longed for Montana's return and cheered for Bono. I felt like the odd man out.

During the season, I met with Coach Walsh, who left the team after my second season, and he gave me some wise advice:

"You cannot take the blame for everything that goes wrong with the 49ers. Don't be the willing scapegoat."

He said each player must account for his own actions and that people will gladly allow others to take blame for their mistakes. Walsh opened my eyes to see that I cheated people out of their own growth when I shouldered their responsibility.

Montana wasn't ready to start the 1992 season, so head coach George Seifert made me the starter. This time I took advantage of the situation and put together a terrific season. I relaxed and we went 15–3 as I won the NFL's Most Valuable Player award. But losing to the Dallas Cowboys in the conference finals was a bitter way to end the season.

As the next season approached, Montana regained his health and there was talk he would be the starter.

When the news broke, I missed all of the controversy because I was studying for my law exams at BYU. Montana solved the problem by signing with the Kansas City Chiefs.

During the 1993 season we put up more impressive numbers but lost to the Cowboys a second straight year, again, one step away from the Super Bowl.

The frustration of 49er fans mounted.

AP/Joe Puglies

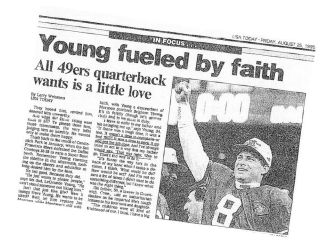

Mike Powell/All Sports

Eric Risberg/All Sports

AP/ Susan Ragan

My personal frustrations boiled over during a 1994 loss to Philadelphia after Coach Seifert benched me. When I came out, we started screaming at each other. I told him I was sick of taking all the blame. It was an unusual outburst for me. Seifert and I cooled off later and apologized to each other. The game marked a turning point for the team. A third straight year we met Dallas in a winner-to-the-Super Bowl game, this time on our home field.

Early interceptions boosted us to a 21–0 lead, and we held off the Cowboys' second-half comeback for the 38–28 win. Overjoyed, I ran a victory lap around Candlestick Park to cherish the moment and share it with the fans.

SPORTS
GHOSTBUSTERS!

The Oakland Tribune.
Super Niners
S.F. dethrones Dallas in its drive for No. 5

SPORTING GREEN
■ The 49ers are overwhelming 17½-point favorites against San Diego in the Super Bowl ■ An emotional Steve Young silences any talk that he can't win the big one ■ Dallas' 3 turnovers give S.F. 21-0 lead after only 4½ minutes

From Mud to Majesty
Chargers rally, stun Steelers   Sky-high 49ers beat Dallas

AP/ Lenny Ignelzi

When it came time to play the San Diego Chargers in Super Bowl XXIX, I had found peace with myself and my role as a football player.

Some might not believe this, but I would have felt successful even if we lost. To play in a Super Bowl after all I'd been through was satisfying enough. The season provided a special gift by showing me I didn't

AP/ Eric Rosberg

San Jose Mercury

AP/ Doug Mills

need to win the "Big One" to find true happiness. I didn't need to compare myself to Montana or McMahon. The only person I had to compare myself to was me.

I felt unusually calm before the Super Bowl and savored the sights, sounds, and emotions.

In a magical 60 minutes, our team displayed the power of perfect teamwork in a 49–26 win.

The victory brought pure joy. I wish every athlete who has swallowed bitter defeat could taste such sweetness.

Many people gave speeches in our locker room. When my turn came, with a hoarse voice and tears flowing, I thanked everyone for making a personal commitment to the season.

We were from different backgrounds, different races and different religions. For a special season, however, we found a oneness in purpose.

Hours after the game interviews ended and the
lights at Miami's Joe Robbie Stadium went black, I
shuffled out of the dressing room and into a limousine
where my agent Leigh was waiting.

We hugged for a moment.

"We did it! We finally did it," I said.

Emotionally and physically drained, I felt light-
headed in the car. I leaned over and threw up on Leigh's
shoes. We joked later that it wasn't exactly the thank
you that my advisor and friend deserved.

The car took us to a hotel where more than 40 of
my family and friends, those who were most important
in my life, awaited my arrival.

I looked faint, which worried some people. An
ambulance was called. Medics ordered me to lie
down and put a needle in my arm to pump in fluids
because I was dangerously dehydrated. Other friends
who stopped by to congratulate me were brought to
my bedside. It was a strange way to end such a
memorable day.

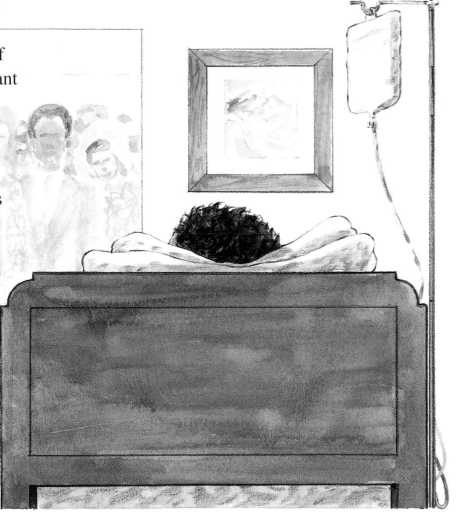

The season following our Super Bowl victory was disappointing for my teammates and the fans. Injuries on our 1995 team, including a midseason operation on my throwing shoulder that kept me out five weeks, made the season difficult.

Still, we made the playoffs thanks to many courageous performances by my teammates. I returned to action in time for the playoffs, but we were knocked out by Green Bay at home.

It felt strange not to play the Cowboys again. Still, I could look at myself in the mirror and know that I did the best I could.

As long as I play football, I will dream of playing in another Super Bowl. Critics will say that until I win a certain number of Super Bowls I am not a success. But that doesn't mean anything to me anymore.

After I retire from football, I look forward to concentrating on other things, such as having my own family and being the best attorney I can be.

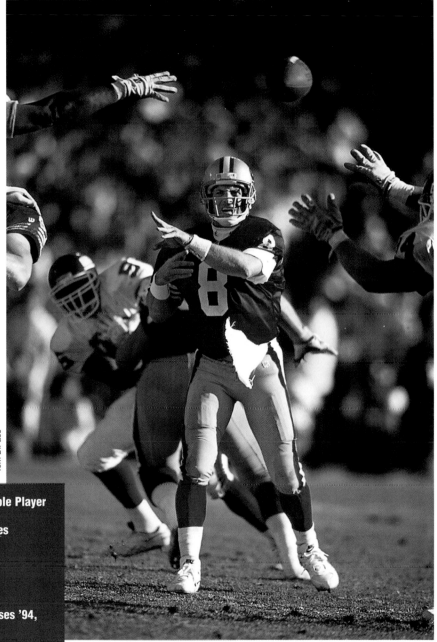

Tom DiPace

- Super Bowl XXIX Most Valuable Player

- Super Bowl record 6 TD passes

- Four-time NFL passing leader

- NFL MVP in 1994, '92

- NFL leader in touchdown passes '94, '93, '92

- Pro Bowl QB, '94, '93, '92

- 49ers all-time rushing quarterback

People will say being a Super Bowl MVP marks the height of my success. I disagree. One game is not the measure of a lifetime.

Success can mean many things to many people. For some students a "C" grade is a success. For some hospital patients simply walking is a great accomplishment.

My advice is to compare yourself only to yourself.

I wrote my definition for success in my high school yearbook. For me the words still stand true today.

Finding success, even in the smallest victories, is what keeps us all forever young at heart.

AP/Paul Sakuma

"To dream and strive for those dreams. To enjoy victory and grow stronger from defeat. To live life to its fullest and fill other lives with joy . . . that is success."

STEVE YOUNG 1980